# My (Most Excellent) Pet Project

Karen McCombie
Lydia Monks

WALKER BOOKS
AND SUBSIDIARIES
LONDON • BOSTON • SYDNEY • AUCKLAND

My name is **Indie Kidd**, and here are three things I think are very cool:

So when my teacher (Miss Levy) set us a project to do this term, I decided pretty quickly to do mine on pets.

I was fourth in my class to write my project title on the board, after Stevie Hughes (who's doing **Why Skateboards Are cool**), and Bradley McDonald (**The History of crisps**), and my brainy best friend Fee (**The Best Big Words I Know And What They Mean**).

My Pet Project

What I wrote on the board was just **My Pet Project**, but now that I've finished, I'm so pleased with it that I'm going to call it **My (Most Excellent) Pet Project**, only with the **Most Excellent** bit in brackets so I don't look is if I'm big-headed or anything.

(Please keep your fingers crossed that Miss Levy thinks it's most excellent too and gives me a good mark!)

By the way, if I sometimes end up talking about stuff apart from pets, it's just that being an animal addict, I can't stop myself. And if you're an animal addict too, I'm sure you won't mind me rabbiting (ha!) on about:

meerkats

and

baby duck-billed platypuses
from time to time.

Oh, and I had to let Dylan have his own section at the end – he said that lots of people love animals but aren't allowed a pet, which is true. And because Dylan is one of those people, I thought he was exactly the right person to write something. I hope you like **How to fake a pet and stuff** as much as I do.

(And a Woof, miaow, squeak and squawk to all the pets out there!)

# My (Most Excellent) Pet Project

## INDIE KIDD

CONTENTS

## Part 1

### MY PETS

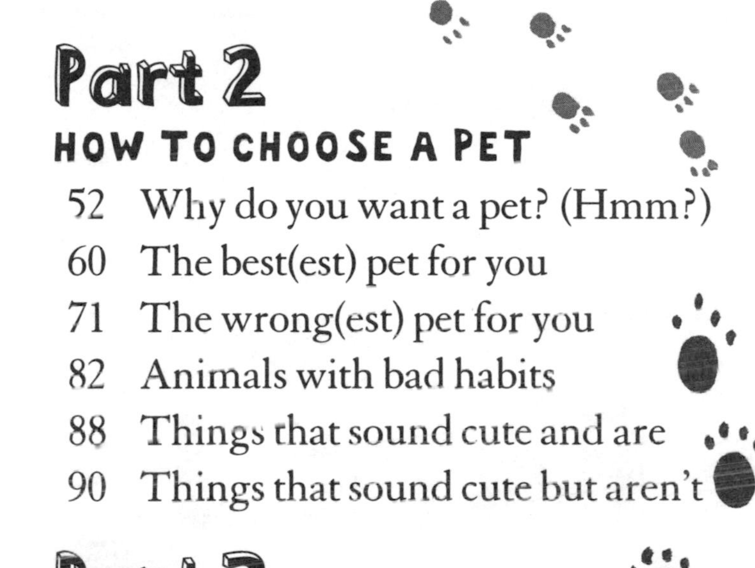

# Part 2

## HOW TO CHOOSE A PET



# Part 3

## HOW TO MAKE A PET FEEL AT HOME



## DYLAN'S BIT

Part 1
MY
PETS

# Smile*, please!
## (*tricky, if you're a fish)

Here are some of my favourite photos of my furry/scaly best friends...

Me and Kenneth, when we were much tiddlier.

Mum plays spot-the-difference with Smudge.

Ever feel like you're being watched?

Dibbles at bathtime.

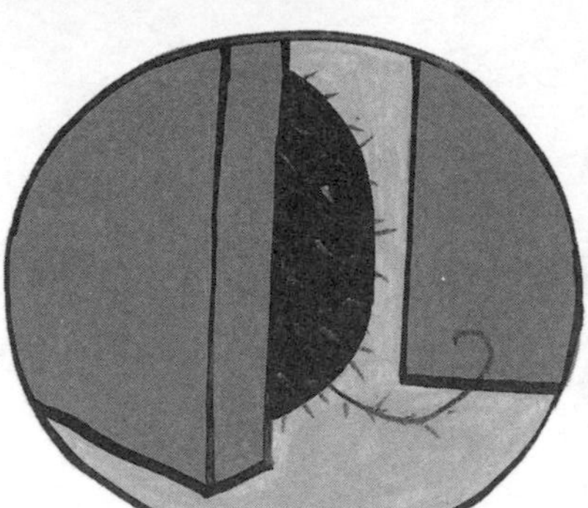

I know for a fact that my dog Dibbles and step-brother Dylan aren't related, but...

Our lodger Caitlin and George, in total harmony - I don't think.

A very unusual pose for Smudge, i.e. she is not asleep for once.

The dogs taking my best(est) friend Soph for a walk.

It's a hard life, being one of our pets...

My other best(est) friend Fee "admiring" Five-and-a-half's lacy look (i.e. fin-rot).

# My gorgeous pets

When I did this thing called a Family Map at school, I stuck on photos of Mum, Caitlin our lodger, Dad, my step-mum Fiona, my nine-year-old step-brother Dylan and all of my pets.

A boy in my class called Jamie Ross (who picks his nose when he thinks no one is looking) said that wasn't right: Caitlin wasn't my sister or anything, and pets weren't people, so I shouldn't say they were all part of my family.

Duh!

If Dylan can be part of my family 'cause his mum married my dad, then I didn't see why other people (and things) that I live with and love can't be called family too.

My teacher, Miss Levy, totally agreed with me, and we did a whole class discussion on different types of families and what makes you happy.

That showed Jamie Ross, who stayed very quiet and huffy through the talk. (Though I did find a dried-in bogey on my schoolbag when I got home, so he might have got his own back on me...)

Anyway, here is a guide to the lovely, **gorgeous** pets I own (or who own me), in the order they came to live with us.

# All about Kenneth

Kenneth was my very first pet. Mum always laughs when she remembers him as a puppy – she says he was like a fluffy black mitten.

I can't remember him being little, mainly 'cause I was pretty little at the time too (see my Photo Album pic!).

Mum got him from the Paws For Thought Rescue Centre as a present for me, around the time my dad left home (can't remember that, either).

Kenneth had belonged to a family who

thought having a puppy would be cute, till they realised dogs can't do stuff like wipe very muddy paws on doormats, or open their own tins of food.

Getting technical, Kenneth is a Scottie dog, which is short for Scottish highland terrier. People get him muddled up with similar sorts of terrier, but it's pretty easy to tell the difference.

Kenneth is mostly a nice, normal and only sometimes slightly grumpy dog. I say mostly, because there are times

when he
acts an awful
lot like a cat.

We have no idea why he might want to act like a cat – maybe he grew up around one when he was a tiny pup and had a crush on it or something.

If you want proof of his kitty-ness,

here goes:

- he does more of a **Meee-howwwwl!** than a WOOF
- he once got stuck up a tree
- he prefers Smudge's food to the stuff George and Dibbles eat
- last week I caught him trying to arch his back at a growly Rottweiler in the park, the way cats do when they're trying to scare something away.

My step-brother Dylan – who was with us at the time – said that Kenneth looked way cool, like a Ninja Scottie. I don't know whether the growly Rottweiler thought Kenneth was a Ninja or cool; I think he just worried that he was weird. Either way, he padded off with his tail between his legs.

Despite reckoning that he is a cat, Kenneth is very smart. He can tell the sound of my dad and my step-mum Fiona's car from all other cars (he sits bolt upright and perks one ear up like a flag).

He magically knows when it's going rain (and refuses to budge for a walk – unlike George, Dibbles and me, who end up getting soaked).

The funniest smart thing Kenneth does is watch TV shows with animals in them. His favourites are wildlife documentaries and those shows where people send in clips of their dogs surfboarding or whatever.

Whenever animals appear on the TV, Kenneth gets all excited and sits about a centimetre from the screen, making odd **hmm-nimmm**-y sort of whining noises.

It's very entertaining, except for the fact that his hairy head gets in the way of us humans watching our favourite programmes.

Still, we can soon fix that, with the bribe of a catnip mouse to play with.

I ♡ Kenneth because ...

he snuffles his nose under my hand when he wants a pat

I think I was around six when Smudge moved in with us. By that time she was already about a hundred in cat years, Mum said. That's because:

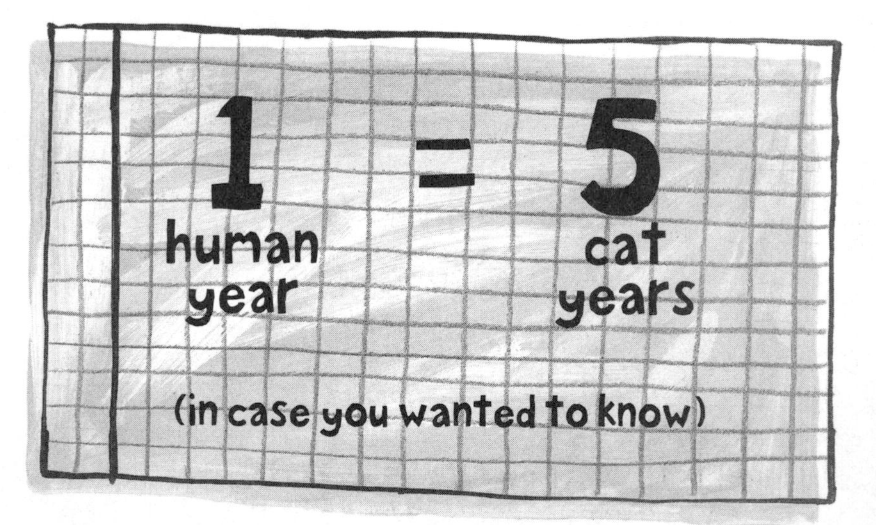

Mum brought her back from the Rescue Centre because Smudge was so old and skinny and frail that she thought it would be

a) hard to re-home Smudge, and
b) nice to give such a grand old lady a lovely, comfy time with us for the last little chunk of her life.

So far, that last little chunk of life has gone on for four years (or twenty, in cat years).

You know, it's funny, but as soon as Smudge set paw in our place, it was as if she'd had a catty makeover. Straight away she put on weight, looked as if she'd started using conditioner on her fur (so ***glossy***!) and suddenly seemed a lot less ancient than she had before.

I mean, she's still old, of course, and her main hobby is sleeping, but she's lovely to have around. Right from the start, Kenneth never minded her – I'm sure mainly because he thought she was just a fluffy, slightly purry cushion.

Actually, we have to be very careful when visitors come, as they do tend to sit on Smudge, which is not very good for her, and not very good for the visitor. The quickest way for Smudge to let a visitor know they have sat on her is to stick her claws in their bottom –

Yeooowww!

Dylan worries a lot about Smudge getting squashed by careless visitors. Lately he came up with a couple of ideas to make her more visible. I quite liked the flashing-light collar (you can buy them for dogs, for walks on dark winter evenings), but spray-painting her with neon-pink hair colour was a bit much.

Dylan was kind of disappointed: he'd spent three weeks' pocket money on the can of Crazy Colour.

Still, it didn't go to waste; our lodger Caitlin bought it from him. She sprayed all our fringes pink for fun, and then bet me and Dylan we wouldn't dare walk with her to the pet shop to buy the flashing collar. We did, and got some seriously strange looks.

Ha!

Anyway, the flashing-light collar didn't turn out to be such a good idea. I guess that for Smudge, all that flashing must have meant it was like trying to fall asleep at a disco.

As soon as she could, she yanked it off her head and dumped it. (We found it last week, flashing in the garden.)

I guess Smudge just wants to take her chances at getting sat on. And maybe we just need to put up a big notice at the front door warning visitors that their bottoms are at risk.

## The (almost) true history of

# George

George is a greyhound.

Greyhounds have two speeds: **fast** and **stop**.

They run like long-legged crazy things in the park, then pass the time till their next burst of crazy long-legged running by curling up into surprisingly small balls and snoozing.

People race greyhounds, just like they do horses – only without saddles and jockeys, of course. George is an ex-racing greyhound. He won heaps of races and lots of prizes, till it was time for him to retire in a blaze of glory, on a silk-lined doggy bed, with a lifetime's supply of doggy titbits from a grateful owner.

OK, so that is not exactly true.

One day – when I was about eight – Mum went to work and found a timid-looking George tied with an old bit of rope to the railing outside the Rescue Centre. Attached to the bit of rope there was a note. It said:

This dog is rubbish.
He fell asleep at the starting gate
on his very first race.
I don't want him any more.

Calling animals rubbish makes Mum very annoyed. She was so annoyed, she immediately bought him a glamorous new collar, promised him he could hop, skip or tap-dance instead of running if he wanted to, and brought him home to live with us.

When I first saw him, he was standing all quivery in our hall. He reminded me of a daddy-longlegs (only bigger, of course, and not so easy to fit in a jam jar and shake out of the window).

Unlike our dog Kenneth, he came with no name. At first, I wanted to call him "Bambi", 'cause of his legs and shyness, but then Mum reminded me that the film

*Bambi* is very sad and I realised I might cry every time I called out our new dog's name in the park.

My other best friend, Soph, suggested "Ididl", which sounded very cute (Soph is half-Somalian, and Ididl is her auntie's name).

The only problems were that

Actually, Fee's not been bothered recently by the girl-name/boy-animal thing, as she has called her vicious new boy-cat "Mrs Mumbles". Personally, I think he has got more vicious since he found out "Mrs Mumbles" was his new name…

Anyway, the only other suggestion was "Grrrrr…", which was the name Kenneth seemed to want to call our new dog in those first few days.

But finally, Mum settled on George, after a cousin of hers who was good at long-distance running and nothing much else at school.

Even though he was shy, George settled in very quickly, happily chewing our shoes and deciding that the armchair by the window was his.

He is now the proud owner of a basket full of squeaky, chewy dog toys. The squeaking is very annoying but lots better than having only one unchewed trainer to wear at a time.

I ♥ George because ...

his fur is like velvet to stroke

# One, Two, Three, Four, Five, Five-and-a-half and Brian

Mum says it's very interesting working at the Paws For Thought Rescue Centre, 'cause every week is different, and you never know what sorts of animal are going to be coming in.

Sometimes, it's just what you expect, i.e. a bunch of lost dogs and a cat that's had kittens. Then next thing, you get a pair of lovebirds, a sludge of land snails and a pot-bellied pig.

By the way, Fee told me that the proper name for a group of animals is a **collective noun**.

And she said I shouldn't say "a **bunch** of dogs", 'cause the proper collective noun

is a **pack** of dogs. Then I said fine, but what is the proper collective noun for a group of land snails, then?

She was a bit stuck by that, and Fee hates to be stuck when it comes to words and stuff, so she went and looked it up on her mum's computer. It turns out that it's a **walk** of snails, in case you wanted to know.

And Fee found out some most excellent names for other groups of animals too, while she was at it, such as:

Animal C
http://www.beastlygroups.com
A clowder of cats
A paddling of ducks
A skulk of foxes
An army of frogs
A woop of gorillas
A mischief of mice
A bloat of hippos

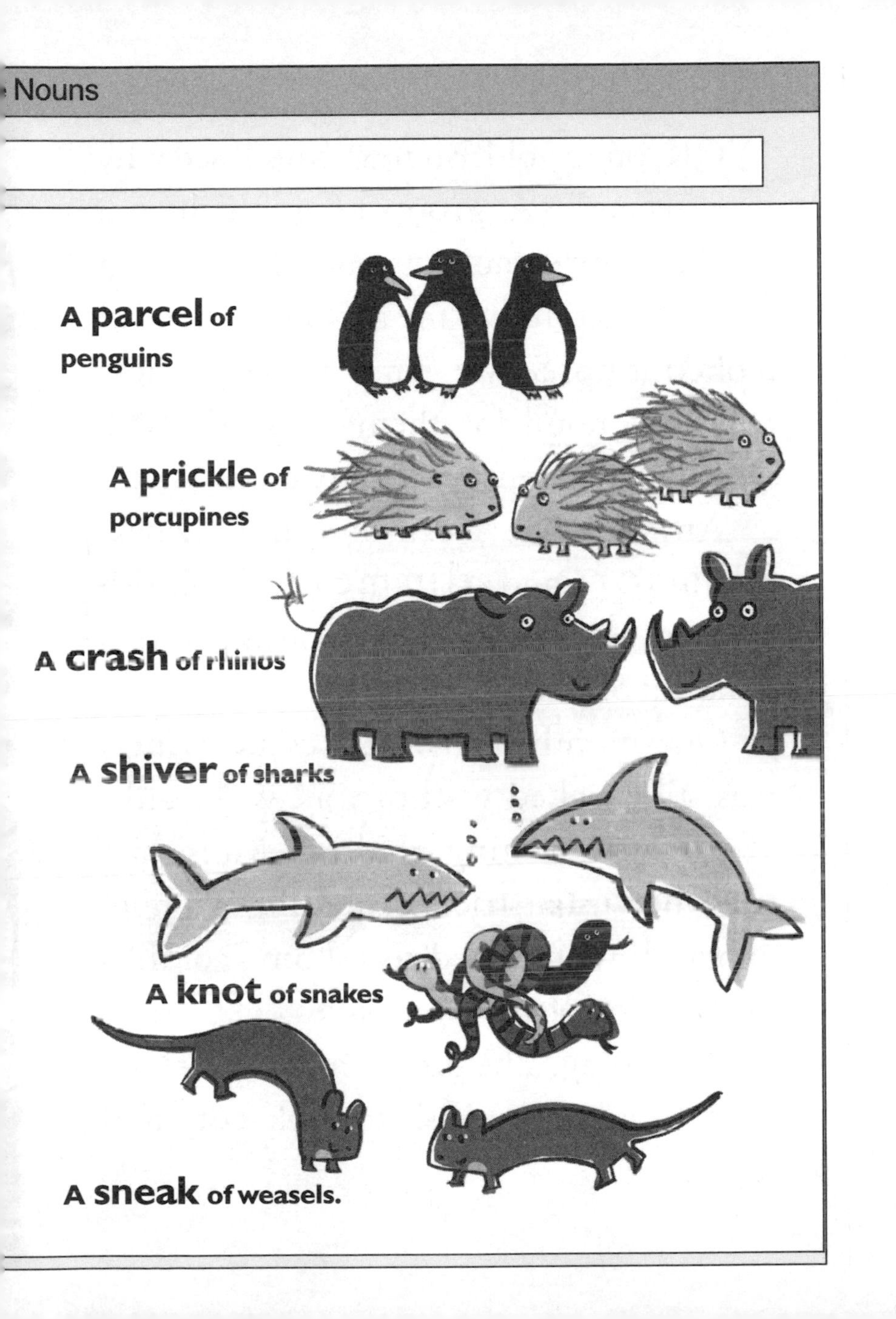
Nouns
A parcel of penguins
A prickle of porcupines
A crash of rhinos
A shiver of sharks
A knot of snakes
A sneak of weasels.

OK, on to goldfish next (you'll see why in a second). A group of goldfish is a shoal, the same as for any fish, which seemed a bit dull to me and Fee when we looked it up. So we came up with a new collective noun for them: a glimmer, which we thought was pretty nice.

Anyway, one week at Mum's work, glimmers and glimmers of goldfish came in, as if suddenly goldfish as pets had gone out of fashion.

One month later, the Rescue Centre was still stacked wall to wall with tanks of patiently waiting goldfish. Mum had tried her usual trick of getting a photo of herself with a hard-to-rehome goldfish in the local newspaper to get some interest going. The problem was, it's really hard to get a goldfish to look cute and

appealing, like a sad-eyed furry dog or whatever.

Anyway, after exactly no new owners came along, everyone who worked at the Rescue Centre – including Mum, Rose the receptionist and Amy the vet – decided to adopt a few fish each.

I don't mean to be horrible, but one goldfish looks a lot like another (except for Five-and-a-half – but that's another story). That's why Mum didn't spend too long choosing her particular fish; she just picked up the nearest tank with five fish

and some fake seaweed in it and relocated it to our living room.

I thought it would be kind of funny just to call them One, Two, Three, Four and Five, and was trying it out on them when I got a bit of a shock: there was a stowaway in the tank! Peeking out from the fake seaweed was a pair of scaredy-cat eyes (OK, scaredy-*fish* eyes).

I shouted for Mum, and we gave the fake seaweed a gentle waggle – and out popped Brian the Angelfish! We got a fleeting look at how pretty and stripy he was, before he popped right back in again.

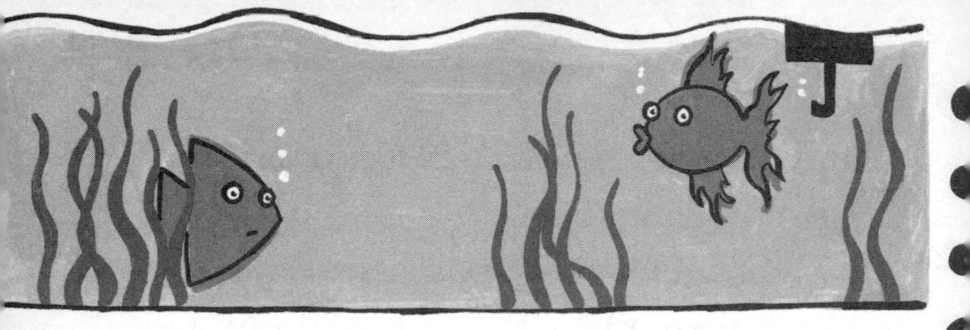

("How did *he* get in there?" I asked Mum at the time. It was a dumb question really. I mean, did I think he'd been dropped in from a spaceship?)

And you know, I can't actually remember why I decided to call him Brian; it just seemed like a good name for a timid angelfish, I guess.

The last fish to join the fishy gang was Five-and-a-half, the only survivor of another glimmer of goldfish who all got fin-rot and died recently. He's better now, but the fin-rot left him with these lacy-look fins and tail. It's kind of pretty for a disease. "It's kind of gross," says Fee, who gets the **collywobbles** every time she looks at him. But then Fee has a problem with damaged goldfish, after finding so many bits of them around her house when her cat Garfield was alive (sadly, the fish weren't).

Still all my fish seem very happy, even shy boy Brian in his fake-seaweed hideout. Except when Caitlin is playing her didgeridoo, of course, which makes the fish tank (and the whole house) vibrate.

Or maybe I've got it wrong and they do like it – from the way they quiver on the spot, it looks as if they might be enjoying a sort of fish jacuzzi.

**I ♥ the fish because …**

**they, er, swim really nicely**

# Dibbles, Dibbles, Dibbles...

Once upon a time, a dog nicknamed the **D.I.B.** (Dog In Black) was the least popular animal at Mum's Rescue Centre.

No one, I mean absolutely no one, was interested in giving him a home. Partly it was 'cause he wasn't very cute-looking (at all), partly 'cause he was a bit thick, and mostly 'cause he wouldn't part with his little blankie, which smelled of dead sardines and boiled cabbage.

I tried very, very hard to help him find a

new owner. I tried making "Please Take Me Home!" posters and putting them up at school. I even tried matchmaking him with my old-lady neighbour Mrs O'Neill.

It took quite a while for me to realise that Mrs O'Neill preferred the idea of a dainty budgie to a large dog with a smelly blankie he didn't want to part with. (**Wow** was he upset when she threw the blankie in the bin!)

And it took a bit longer than that for me to realise this dopey, drooly adorable dog needed a new owner exactly like me.

When Dibbles (which is what I changed his name to) moved in, he was very nervous, even though all the animals were nice to him and Kenneth didn't even growl a single "**Grrrrr...**" in his direction.

You know, Mum said something very **loud** must have happened to Dibbles in his past life, as he is scared of lots of sounds. There are sounds you might expect him to be scared of, like crashes, **bumps**, thumps, **BANGS** and doorbells.

Then there are sounds that scare him that are a bit more surprising, like the toilet being flushed, the kettle boiling, the theme tune to the teatime weather report, and velcro.

(Luckily, he seems to find the booming of Caitlin's didgeridoo

thrumma
rumma
rumma

kind of soothing. He likes to nap on her feet while she parps.)

When a noise scares Dibbles, he usually runs and hides behind unsuitable things. They are unsuitable because they are a lot smaller than him, so he is easy to spot. But sometimes he gets lucky and hides where I can't find him to calm him down.

When I can't find him straight away, there's a simple way to flush him out. I tiptoe round the house, calling out 'Dibbles!' very softly, and then listen very carefully.

As soon as I hear a

**"Thudda-dudda-dudda"**

sound, I know he can't be too far away. (*Boy*, does his short, fat tail make a racket when he thumps it on the ground!)

Dibbles's favourite thing in the world is

his new blankie. But what Dibbles doesn't know is that he has two new blankies. Every now and then when he's snoozing, Mum or I sneak his current blankie away and stick it in the wash, and replace it with a nice, clean one.

Well, we might love Dibbles, but who can love the smell of dead sardines and boiled cabbage?

# Part 2

# HOW TO CHOOSE A PET

# Why do you want a pet? (Hmm?)

Answer the question below to find out if you would be an ace pet-owner.

I want a pet because …

A They are cute and cuddly.
B I'm a bit lonely.
C It would be fun.

The correct answer is: *complicated* (my mum says). The thing is, pets can be cute and cuddly, *and* they can be great if you're a bit lonely, *and* they can be excellent fun.

**BUT ...** before you dive in and get one, you have to think about some very important things, like:

1) Pets can cost a lot of money to buy, and to fix if they get broken (vets' bills can be **huuuuuge**).
2) You might be allergic to some animals (so go hug a friend's hamster and see if you come out in itchy spots or start sneezing, before you go getting one of your own).
3) You have to know someone, like a friend or dog-sitter or whatever, who will look after your pet when you go on holiday (pets aren't good at feeding themselves or cleaning up their own poo).

And that brings us on to a **V.I.P.** (very important point): **all pets POO!** (Especially Dibbles, who needs to poo a lot, for some reason.)

Nobody is very fond of poo, but you can't go all squeamish about it if you want a pet, 'cause everything from the hugest horse to the weeniest gerbil does it and **YOU NEED TO CLEAN IT UP!**

You also need to have lots of time to feed your pet, exercise it (OK, so that's an easy one if you've got a goldfish) and pay it plenty of attention. (See "**How to make a pet feel at home**".)

Actually Caitlin told me a sad story when I was talking to her about writing this bit. She said that when she was a little girl living in Scotland, she and her sister and two brothers pestered their parents for months for a rabbit. Finally, their parents gave in and bought them Bob the bunny, a floppy-eared bundle of cuteness.

For the first week, all the kids fought over who got to cuddle and feed Bob and clean out his hutch (*everyone* wanted to).

The second week, all the kids fought over who got to cuddle and feed Bob and clean out his hutch (*nobody* wanted to).

The third week, Caitlin's parents took him back to the pet shop they'd bought him from, and Caitlin and her sister and brothers felt **guilty** for ages. (She says she still feels **guilty** now, and sometimes wonders where Bob is and whether he's happy. I didn't like to tell her that rabbits live only between five and ten years and, as Caitlin is now nineteen, Bob's bound to be in bunny heaven.)

OK, so now you've read Caitlin's sad story, maybe it's time to answer another pet-type test:

**Tick the boxes that apply to you...**

- ☐ I have enough time to look after a pet.
- ☐ I absolutely promise I'd make sure it was fed/exercised/hugged properly.
- ☐ I am not scared of poo.

If you have ticked all of the above (and really and truly and honestly mean it!), then you are ready for a pet.

So which one should you get? Suitable pets come in all shapes and sizes, to suit big houses and small ones, rambling gardens or the space on top of a chest of drawers.

You could pick something as titchy as a

hamster, or if you have lots of space (and grass), maybe keep a goat. Actually, I've had a bit of a *thing* for goats, ever since Mum told me that there's one type called fainting goats, who freeze or faint when they get a surprise.

Speaking of *things*, Soph has had a bit of a *thing* for pot-bellied pigs ever since one came into the Rescue Centre, but as she lives in a third-floor flat, it's never going to happen. She needs to think about getting something smaller, and something that doesn't need to roll in mud.

So really look at where you live, and think what sort of pet would fit.

# The best(est) pet for you

To help you find the perfect pet, I spoke to my mum and Amy the vet (who works with Mum), and they told me the Top Ten most popular pets around. So I went off and found out some really excellent and interesting facts (I think) about each one…

## 1) Cat

What is it?

A slinky, furry, purry animal, that likes to be stroked and will reward with purrs. (Except for Fee's old cat Garfield, who rewarded her with kisses, and her new one - Mrs Mumbles whose hobby is lunging with claws.)

Weird cat fact:

The average cat has five toes, but there are some called polydactyl cats who have six or even seven toes on their paws. I showed my dad a photo of one on Dylan's computer and he said it looked as if it was wearing furry boxing gloves.

Would it make a good pet?

Cats are happy in all sorts of homes, but not ones beside busy roads, where they might get squashed by passing traffic. (Unfortunately, there aren't enough - OK, <u>any</u> - cat crossings on busy roads.)

## 2) Dog

**What is it?**

A four-legged panting machine. Dogs come in all sizes, shapes, colours and degrees of furriness, but they all pant.

**Weird dog fact:**

From huge dogs to tiny dogs, every one of them is descended from wolves. Sorry, I know this doesn't sound like a particularly weird fact, but it is to me: it's just that I can't believe the whole descended-from-wolves thing when I look at my dopey dog Dibbles. He is about as much like a wolf as Brian our shy Angelfish is like a stealthy shark.

**Would it make a good pet?**

You've got to like going for walks when you've got a dog. Dogs don't like taking the bus or anything.

## 3) Goldfish

### What is it?

A small fish that is gold. Actually, it's more orange, as Dylan pointed out. And no, Dylan, I don't know why they're not called "orangefish."

### Weird goldfish fact:

Goldfish can tell the time, sort of. Everyone always thinks that goldfish have no memory at all, but some fish in an experiment pressed a lever whenever their fishy tummies rumbled, which happened to be at the exact same time every day.

### Would it make a good pet?

Goldfish are very easy pets to look after, and you don't need to go out in the rain to walk them. But they still poo, don't forget, and you'll have to clean their tank out.

## 4) Hamster

**What is it?**

A fluffball, with tiny little feet.

**Weird hamster fact:**

Hamsters tend to be gentle, unless you surprise them, or wake them up suddenly. Then they get very grumpy indeed and might nip you.

**Would it make a good pet?**

Hamsters make very nice pets; the only problem is that they sleep during the day ("That's called being nocturnal," says Fee). So if you wake them up for a play, expect nips. Or maybe you could turn nocturnal too (except that might make you miss mealtimes and your favourite TV programmes, so it's maybe not such a great idea...).

## 5) Gerbil

What is it?
Like a cross between a mouse and a rat. Lives in deserts in the wild.

Weird gerbil fact:
When a gerbil is suddenly excited, or gets surprised, it drums its back feet on the ground. (Surprise a whole group of gerbils, and it could sound quite funky!)

Would it make a good pet?
Yes, and you don't even need to live in a desert – a nice roomy cage will do fine for your gerbilly friend. And another thing: I did my gerbil research on Dylan's computer and he found this brilliant American website where you can order "I ♡ gerbil" hoodies, mugs and even thongs! Perfect, if you're a little bit nuts about your pet.

## b) Guinea pig

### What is it?

Not a pig, that's for sure. It's a furry rodent from Brazil and Peru and other South American places. Baby guinea pigs can survive on their own after only five days.

### Weird guinea-pig fact:

Folk doctors in the Andes mountains believed that when guinea pigs were pressed up against a sick person, they'd squeak when near to the place where the health problem was.

### Would it make a good pet?

Definitely. Guinea pigs are very friendly and playful. Plus guinea pigs are less easy than hamsters and gerbils to squish accidentally with too-hard hugs.

# 7) Budgie

## What is it?

A bird that comes in lots of seaside-rock colours, and can be trained to talk. It weighs about the same as a packet of crisps.

## Weird budgie fact:

My old-lady neighbour, Mrs O'Neill, has a budgie called Archie, which can do something pretty weird: whenever she puts the hoover on he rocks back and forth on his perch, as if he's the one cleaning the floor.

## Would it make a good pet?

As long as you don't mind the tweeting. And you have to be kind and let them fly outside their cage from time to time. Just make sure that happens in a room with no open windows - and no cats with open mouths.

## 8) Rabbit

**What is it?**

A floppy-eared vegetarian. You can get weeny little rabbits, or great big ones, like the **Flemish Giant Rabbit**, which is about twice the size of the average cat. (Dylan says he'd quite like to watch an average cat meet a **Flemish Giant Rabbit**, and see how confused it would get.)

**Weird rabbit fact:**

The position of their eyes allows rabbits to see behind them without turning their heads.

**Would it make a good pet?**

Mostly, rabbits live in hutches and runs outside, but you can train them to be house pets – they'll learn to use litter trays, just like cats!

## 9) Rat

### What is it?

An animal that makes lots of people go "yuck!". That's a shame, 'cause rats are just like bigger gerbils really, and people seem to like them OK. (Well, maybe not my step-mum Fiona. I don't understand how anyone can't like animals. It's like saying chocolate is yucky, which is mad.)

### Weird rat fact:

Way, way, way back in the 1300s, lots of people died of the plague. People still say it was caused by black rats. BUT it's now known that it was actually the fleas on the black rats that carried the plague germs. So there.

### Would it make a good pet?

Even though they're a lot (lot) smaller, rats are smarter than cows, horses and some dogs (especially Dibbles).

## 10) Mouse

### What is it?

A tiny, dainty little rodent that makes lots of people go "Eeeeek!!" when they see one, as if they were terribly scary and carry guns or something.

### Weird mouse fact:

The name for the fear of mice is "musophobia".

### Would it make a good pet?

Not if anyone in your family suffers from musophobia. Apart from that they make very good pets, and are very friendly. They like living with mouse buddies - but don't mix boy mice with girl mice, because they can have babies every three weeks, which is a LOT of mice, no matter how nice and friendly they are.

# The wrong(est) pet for you

As part of my pet project, I asked people in my class to think about what their dream pet would be, and stick their answers in a box.

I didn't expect quite so many weird answers (which all looked suspiciously as if they were written by secret nose-picker Jamie Ross).

But just so you know the type of animals that definitely *wouldn't* make good pets, I did some research on the weirdest ones in there.

## 1) Frog

### What is it?

An amphibian (posh word for an animal that can live in water and on land - Fee had to help me spell that.) Like a toad, but not so knobbly.

### Weird frog fact:

Did you know that in between a tadpole and a fully-grown frog, there's something called a froglet? And some countries have hazard signs to help frogs cross the road. Also, the Gastric Brooding Frog gives birth out of its mouth!

### Would it make a good pet?

They like living in garden ponds, but owning them could make you sad, since neighbourhood cats might like them as a snack. (I bet all the local frogs in ponds near Fee's house had a party when they heard her killer cat Garfield had died.)

## 2) Hedgehog

### What is it?

Spiky. And sort of spooky. (I mean hibernating all winter. How weird is that when you think about it?!)

### Weird hedgehog fact:

Hedgehogs whistle when they are hunting. (Worms and insects must be pretty thick – "Hmm, I wonder what that whistling noise could be? Oh!–" *Gulp*.) And in medieval times, people used to think hedgehogs kept a supply of fruit, stuck on their spines. And another thing: eating fish makes hedgehogs ill.

### Would it make a good pet?

Might get household objects stuck to its spines, like socks and cotton buds. Better as just an interesting visitor to your garden (they like cat food, if you fancy leaving them some nibbles).

## 3) Ant

### What is it?

An insect. A really *strong* insect – an ant can carry twenty times its own body weight. My step-brother Dylan and I left a really big Quaver on the floor near an ant once and it lifted the whole thing away. Try it – it's like a sort of helpful biology experiment. You get to see how strong an ant is, and they get the best picnic ever for them and their mates.

### Weird ant fact:

Some birds deliberately put ants in their feathers, 'cause ants can squirt a kind of acid that keeps other bugs away.

### Would it make a good pet?

No. You would keep losing it. And it's too small for a collar and name tag.

## 4) Alligator

**What is it?**

Scary. OK, it's actually a reptile. An alligator can grow up to 5.5 metres long, which is about the same as me, my friends Soph and Fee and Dylan all lying end to end. (Shudder.)

**Weird alligator fact:**

They have a type of "radar" in their cheeks that can detect ripples in the water, so they know when a snack might be in the area.

**Would it make a good pet?**

Only if you think getting your arms bitten off is good fun.

## 5) Elephant

**What is it?**

One of the biggest mammals going. (Whales are bigger but I haven't seen one close up.)

**Weird elephant fact:**

Elephants actually walk on their tiptoes – their heels are supported by a cushion of fatty tissue. And they use their huge trunks in very delicate ways: they can pick up pins with them; they can curl them round pencils and make marks on paper; and they can use them as snorkels to swim under water like submarines (now that *is* cool!).

**Would it make a good pet?**

Er, no, not unless your mum or dad happened to own a wildlife park. (How brilliant would *that* be?)

## 6) Llama

What is it?

A shaggy-haired animal that comes from the mountains of South America. Sort of like a horse with a camel's head.

Weird llama fact:

When they are happy, llamas hum.

Would it make a good pet?

Perhaps you could teach it to hum a tune, but only if it was in the right (happy) mood. Like all big animals, there would a lot of poo to clear up, so not a great pet, unless you have a *field* as a back garden. (Which I personally don't - boo!)

## 7) Meerkat

### What is it?

"Meerkat" comes from an Afrikaans (South African) word meaning marsh cat. But they don't live near marshes and they aren't cats. They actually come from the mongoose family.

### Weird meerkat fact:

Meerkats eat scorpions by biting off their poisonous tails first. (Smart.) They also have dark rings under their eyes that act like built-in sunglasses. (Cool.)

### Would it make a good pet?

They can be friendly and cute and curious with people - yay! But they like eating insects, scorpions and snakes, which aren't for sale in the pet section of your local supermarket, I don't think.

## 8) Zebra

### What is it?

A horse with stripes. A zebra's stripes are like human fingerprints - no two zebras have exactly the same markings.

### Weird zebra fact:

A zebra can bark like a dog.

### Would it make a good pet?

They can charge at lions and scare them off when they're in a bad mood. So I guess if you had a problem with lions, they'd be quite handy. Otherwise, no.

## 9) Manatee

### What is it?

It's a sea cow. ("And what are sea cows?" asked Dylan when he read the scribbles in my notebook. Nosy.) Sea cows are like giant, blobby seals. They are kind of cute in a not-pretty, Dibbles sort of way.

### Weird manatee fact:

They may be mermaids. Well, it's reckoned that sailors from long ago saw them sitting on rocks in the distance, holding their pups in their "arms" like human mothers, and maybe thought they were some magical half-fish, half-woman creature. (Though not a very pretty woman, obviously.)

### Would it make a good pet?

Nope – you'd need an ocean in your back yard.

## 10) Unicorn

**What is it?**

Not real (see below).

**Weird unicorn fact:**

A male narwhal whale has this freaky long, hollow tooth that spirals from its jaw. In medieval times, Vikings used to sell these narwhal teeth on their trading routes all over Europe. They told the people who bought them that they were magical unicorn horns. (Bet you just thought Vikings were fierce invaders – but obviously they were practical jokers, too!)

**Would it make a good pet?**

Yes, in an imaginary way. (And hey – imaginary animals don't have poo that needs cleaning up.)

# Animals with BAD habits

So animals can't brush their teeth and clean up after themselves. But it gets much worse than that…

Fee's cat Garfield (RIP) had some seriously bad habits.

Knowing your cat is eating the entire population of frogs and goldfish out of your neighbours' garden ponds is bad enough. Finding chewed bits of frogs and goldfish in your slippers and in your schoolbag is a lot worse.

But Fee loved (and misses) Garfield lots, and loves her new cat Mrs Mumbles just as much. Mrs Mumbles has plenty of bad habits too. He (remember, he is a boy) likes to hang off your hand by his claws when you try to stroke him. He doesn't seem to like ankles very much either, and swipes at them at every opportunity.

This makes my dog George's occasional chew on a trainer seem almost cute. And Dibbles's habit of rifling through the food-recycling bin and eating onion skin and banana peel downright funny (unless he sicks them up right after, of course).

But even Garfield and Mrs Mumbles sound adorable next to this lot...

✸ When a **frog** swallows, its eyes sink into its skull to help push the food down its throat. (Just imagine your little brother doing that next time you sit down to tea.)

✸ **Bush babies** wee on their paws to give them extra grip. (Dylan says maybe someone could invent tiny rubber gloves so they don't have to.)

✸ The **Californian condor** (a kind of vulture) wees on its feet to clean them.

✸ **Horned lizards** squirt blood out of their eyes. (Yewwww...)

✸ The world's largest snake is the **anaconda,** which can swallow a deer whole. (At least other animals in the jungle can get a laugh at how stupid it must look.)

The **bombardier beetle** defends itself by "exploding". It makes two chemicals that react together with a **POP!**, and out comes a cloud of smelly red spray.

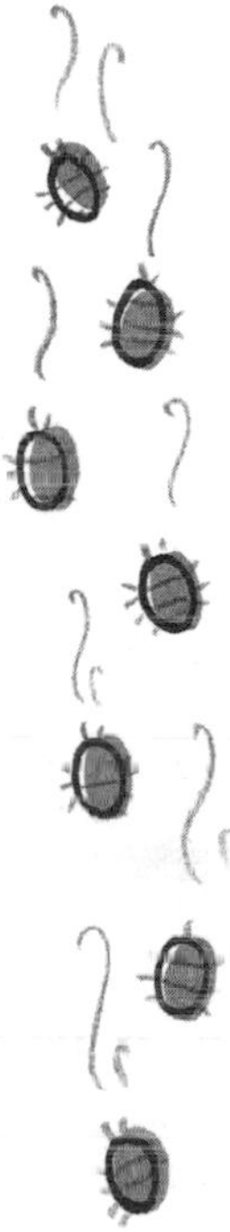

Instead of weeing, **woodlice** get rid of toxins by passing a whiffy gas through their scales. (At least they're so small you probably wouldn't be able to smell it.)

**Geckos** lick their own eyes to keep them clean.

A **vampire bat** drinks the equivalent of five people's blood in a year.

A **dung beetle** makes its home in poo. (Now your messy room probably doesn't look so bad.)

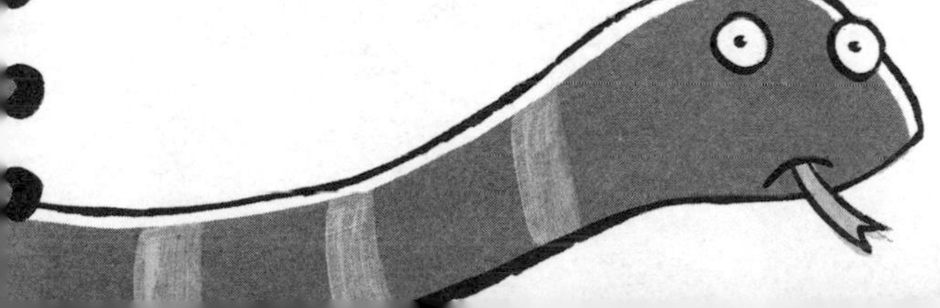

# Things that sound cute and are

OK, so these aren't strictly speaking pets, but if you're as mad on animals as I am, these'll make you go "*Ahhh...*".

- **Fingerling:** A baby fish.
- **Kit:** A baby fox.
- **Puggle:** A baby duck-billed platypus.

✸ **Mousebird:** A tiny Kenyan bird with long tail feathers, that scampers along branches like a mouse. (Cute!)

✸ **Puddle clubs:** Groups of butterflies gathered round puddles to drink.

✸ **Wandering whistling duck:** A brown duck that has a whistling call, and whose wings make a whistling sound when they flap.

# Things that sound cute but aren't

These animals have names that make you feel warm and fuzzy inside – till you see them (shudder). Trust me, you will never want one of these as a pet…

* **Mudpuppy:** A brown, flat-headed salamander that lives in streams in North America. The knobbly bits with red frills around its neck are positively icky.
* **Blue-tongued skink:** Looks like the result of welding the head of a snake onto

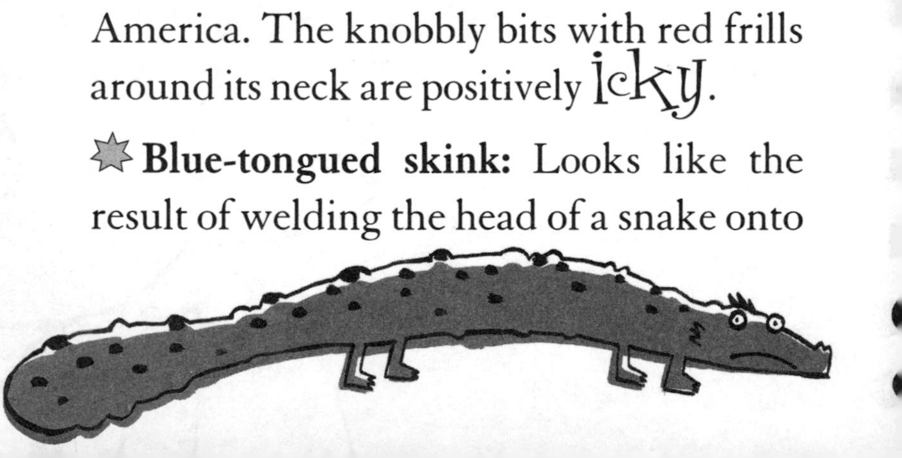

the body of a stripy lizard. And has a blue tongue. Hmm. You might come across one in Indonesia. Then again you might not want to.

✵ **Brown booby:** A not-very-pretty, big, gangly bird from the Gulf of Mexico. It's got a sort of comedy beak that's too big for its head, and get this: its eyes look like part of the beak!

✵ **Three-toothed Caroline:** A small, blobby bit of plankton, found in the ocean. Not particularly toothy, despite the name. And did you know that scientists who discover new species of animals or plants sometimes like to name them after their wives?

If I were Caroline, the plankton scientist's wife, I don't know how chuffed I'd really be to have a small blobby thing named after me...

**Spotted wobbegong:** Hang about in the sea around Australia and you might come across this knobbly, flat, pizza-shaped type of shark with seriously weird frills around its mouth.

**Pink fairy armadillo:** Comes from Argentina. Looks like a giant acorn crossed with a cotton-wool ball, with legs.

# Part 3

# HOW TO MAKE A PET FEEL AT HOME

HOME SWEET HOME

# Settling your pet

For an animal, moving in to a new home must feel super-strange. Help make it as un-strange as you can by making sure your pet has all the stuff it needs before you take it home.

That should be stuff like food and water bowls, leads, collars, name-tags, litter trays and toys (depending on the size and shape of the pet you are expecting).

Most important is its bed, 'cause that's where your pet is going to feel safe and snuggly. For some pets, that's going to

mean a cage or a tank or a hutch, and for some it's a cosy basket or bed it can call its own.

"Or a jam jar," Dad said, last Sunday, when he was driving me home to Mum's and I was reading out my notes for this section to him.

"A jam jar?" I asked, confused.

It turned out that the only pet Dad had ever had as a kid was a **bee**.

"Not a *full* jar," Dad added, as if I had any intention of getting myself a bee and trapping it in a jar filled with strawberry jam. "But you know, you must *always* remember to put holes in the lid."

It turned out that Dad *hadn't* put holes in the lid of *his* jar, and so by the next morning his pet bee had died through lack of oxygen. (It would probably have died happier drowning in strawberry jam.)

Anyway, let's forget about (dead) bees and get back to getting your new arrival settled.

If you already have other pets, you need to introduce the new pet very carefully.

Your dog might think it is being very friendly, coming up for a sniff and a welcoming lick, but to a guinea pig that must feel like the last few seconds before it is devoured by a foul-breathed mega-monster.

Keep animals well away from each other, and let them check each other out from a distance, before you slowly introduce them.

Also, you might be desperate to cuddle and play with your pet straight away, but your new pet might not feel the same. For the first few days it will be thinking, "Where am I?", "Who are you?" and, if it's very small, "What is that big thing with five wiggly pointy bits on it and why does it keep coming towards me?" (i.e. your hand).

Your pet isn't going anywhere (unless

you leave the cage door open: see the "**Looking after your pet**" section next), so take your time and let it get used to you nice and slowly.

In no time at all, you and your new pet will be best(est) buddies...

Treats of food are a very good way of bribing your new pet to like you. (Hey, maybe you could train your dog to offer titbits of apple to your guinea pig! Then again, the dog would probably just eat the apple first, and then all the guinea pig would see would be a mega-monster with slightly nicer breath coming to eat it.)

# Looking after your pet

You don't have to be **super-smart** to figure out that you must give your pet the right food, and the right amount of food.

And you don't have to be **super-smart** to figure out that you have to make sure your pet has the right sort of exercise, like big walks (if it's a dog), or a catnip mouse to play with (if it's a, er, cat), or just interesting things to run through and around (if it's a gerbil or something).

OK, so proper food and exercise will keep your pet nice and healthy, but I thought maybe pet-owners should know some first-aid stuff too. So I went and had some juice and biscuits and a chat with Amy the vet from the Paws For Thought Rescue Centre to find out more.

I asked, "Can you tell me all the **ill things** that can happen to every kind of pet and how a pet-owner could fix them?"

Amy said that it took her seven years at vet school to learn all the **ill things** that can happen to every pet and how to fix them.

Hmm... I realised that I would be seventeen by the time she finished telling me everything, and my Pet Project would be *way* too long and *very* late.

Instead she gave me some handy hints to keep your pet safe, which are much shorter...

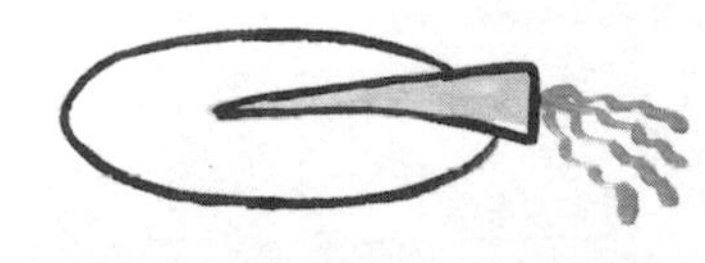

# YOUR PET:

# CAT

## THE DANGER:

## Other cats

Cats don't like their kitty neighbours much, and don't like sharing space with them. When a kitty neighbour does stray into their territory, that's when cats can get into a **yeoooowwwwwlllling**, hisssssssing, furry ball of teeth and claws and fighting.

If your cat comes home with a bite or scratch, chuck some salt into warm water, and dab it onto the bitten/scratched bit. Your cat will not like it much ('cause it's a bit nippy), but salt helps kill the bugs that get into bites and scratches. This is very easy to do and a very handy thing to know, because if the bite or scratch gets infected, then you'll have to go to the vet for antibiotics. Then your parents will be in a bad mood because they're worrying about the cat, and grumbly because they have to pay a big vet bill, when maybe just a (very cheap) bit of salt and warm water would have done the trick if anyone had thought of it at the time.

## YOUR PET:
# DOG

## THE DANGER:
Socks

Dogs will eat pretty much everything, but Amy says dogs come into vets' surgeries lots and lots of times with sore tummies and not being able to eat or poo, and when the vet does an X-ray, it turns out it's socks. Who knows why dogs choose socks in particular to munch on (maybe to them, the whiff of feet is like the smell of toffee popcorn to us).

All you can <u>really</u> do is make sure everyone in your family knows they must keep their socks safely in the drawer or the laundry basket and not inside the dog.

(Amy says that when she was a trainee vet, a dog came into her surgery **bleeping**. She panicked and consulted all the other vets. They came in one by one and stared at the **bleeping** dog, and couldn't think of anything to do but X-ray it. One X-ray later it turned out that the dog had swallowed its owner's watch and the alarm had gone off.)

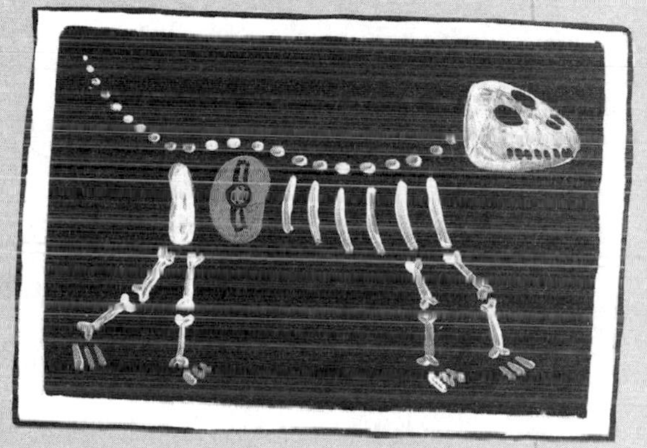

## YOUR PET:

# HAMSTER/ GERBIL/ SMALL FURRY THING

## THE DANGER:

## Doors

That's cage doors, to be precise. Amy says that when you have been feeding or playing with your small furry thing, you **must, must, must** always remember to close the cage door, which people often forget to do. An open cage door is not healthy for your pet because it will think, "Hmm ... wonder what's out here?" Then it will disappear in your house, which is like the size of the universe to a small furry thing, and you might not be able to find it ever again. Except maybe sad and dead behind the washing machine when you move house years later.

Sophie said that when she was little, the fat pet hamster at her nursery got out of its cage just before the summer holidays, 'cause someone forgot to close the door. It turned up two months later, looking more like a mouse on a very strict diet than a cuddly round hamster. They think it survived on spiders, fluff and playdough. (It was very, VERY glad to get back to its cage, and to the bulging bowlfuls of seeds and apple.)

## YOUR PET:
# BUDGIE
## THE DANGER:
Windows

If you are a kind owner, and let your bird come out of its cage to fly around from time to time, you have to be very careful about windows. OPEN ones are bad, because your bird will fly out and be lost for ever. But CLOSED windows are dangerous too, 'cause birds don't really understand what windows are and might spot the trees and sky and and think, "Ooh ... I fancy flying over there and having a little loo– **OOOF!**"

Thunking into a glass window is not much fun for a tiny birdie, so maybe draw the curtains or pull down the blind during a fly-around to avoid any unexpected **splats**.

# YOUR PET: FISH

## THE DANGER: Cats

Cats can't help it – they think fish are a cross between a toy and a snack. They don't mean to be mean (unless they are Fee's cats Garfield and Mrs Mumbles) – it's just a natural instinct, like it's Caitlin's natural instinct to play the didgeridoo.

Anyway, there's no harm in a cat entertaining itself by staring at fish swishing around a tank.

The problem comes when you catch it dipping a paw into the water. Or, worse still, sitting next to an empty tank, chewing.

So if you want to have a pet cat **AND** pet fish, you have to get the sort of tank that has a **LID** on it. Either that or buy a muzzle for your cat.

After Amy told me all that stuff, I asked her when you *should* panic and decide to take your pet to the vet.

She said you should definitely pay your vet a visit if your pet has obviously been hurt; if it is barfing a lot (but not just cat-fur-ball barfing); if it keeps having diarrhoea; if it stops eating and drinking for more than a couple of days; and if it goes all **limp** and **floppy** and miserable and doesn't cheer up after a few days, even when you wiggle its favourite toy around and try to tickle its tummy.

You should definitely **NOT** rush your pet to the vet in the middle of the night claiming it's got a sudden, scary, hard growth on its hind leg without checking closer first. This is Amy's favourite vet story ever: she examined this big, hairy Alsatian very carefully as its worried owners looked on … and found that the sudden, scary hard growth was actually a sticky boiled sweet that their dog must have sat on. How embarrassing was that?

Still, paying a vet to snip a sweet out of your pet's fur in the middle of the night is probably a lot less embarrassing than looking at your wrist, and suddenly realising where your lost watch has gone, as your dog **bleeps** in the background.

# Things you must **never** do to your pet

## Give it a name that is embarrassing to say in public

Giving your pet a very silly or rude name might be funny for five minutes, but it isn't a good idea. Your neighbours will pull **urgh** faces when you say it out loud, and it won't be nice when the vet comes into the crowded surgery waiting room and says, "Smelly? Is there someone with a rabbit called Smelly here?"

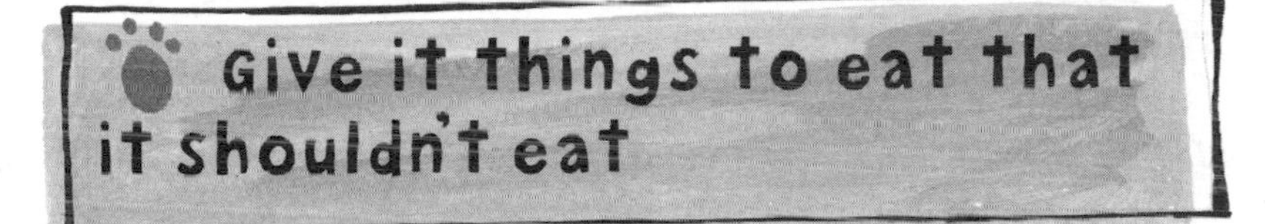

## Give it things to eat that it shouldn't eat

Pets can get very ill if you give them stuff to eat that they shouldn't have – even something that doesn't sound too bad. Giving your dog chocolate might seem like a laugh – but it won't be much fun when he gets a sore tummy and you have to clean up the mess.

## Leave tiny kids alone with it

The trouble is, little kids don't realise that pets can break. They don't get it that animals aren't toys, so it's best to watch them like crazy and make sure they don't dangle your hamster by its ears 'cause they like that funny squeaking noise it makes when they do.

## Dress it up in stupid clothes

OK, OK, I did this to Dibbles once, but I feel very guilty about it.

## Dress it up in stupid clothes and take a photo of it

Yes, I admit it, I did this too – but I was trying to win a competition in the local paper. I promise I will NEVER make my poor darling dumb dog look even *more* dumb ever again...

# Things you must **always** do for your pet

## Look after it ... even if you're tired and not in the mood

Imagine if your mum or dad or whoever decided to hang out with their chums, mooch around reading magazines and listening to music, ignored you and never gave you your tea or a hug. How rubbish would *that* be?

## Not take it for granted ... just 'cause it's always there and doesn't say anything

Even if you're 100% busy, make it a rule never to pass your pet without saying hello, or patting it (if it's pattable).

## Love it ... 'cause you're it's best friend

Your pet might not be able to understand "I love you" in words, but caring for it is the simplest way of letting it know you, er, care!

Dylan's
bit
HOW TO FAKE
A PET [AND STUFF]

Hello I'm **Dylan**. 
I'm Indie Kidd's step-brother I am nine and I love animals too but I'm not allowed to have any because my mum comes up with lots of reasons like too much hair everywhere and allergies and what-do-you-do-if-you-go-on-holiday reasons but really I know it's 'cause she just doesn't like them much.

(By the way I'm very good at maths but not so good at writing because although I'm OK at spelling I always get muddled about where I'm meant to put commas so I just don't bother. Sorry I hope it doesn't make

19+17+21+42=99

this bit too hard to read.)

I know that it's not just my mum and that LOTS of people like animals but have parents or carers or whoever who say NO you can't have a pet that's a very bad idea.

So I asked Indie if I could write something about that and she said yes as long as you don't write anything stupid Dylan because I want to get a good mark for this project.

Anyway I have been thinking about this lots and I have some ideas about how you can try to persuade your parents that pets are ace and that you will be an ace pet-owner.

And I have an idea about how to fake a pet which is kind of fun and could make

16 + 4



Dylan is cool

your parents feel so guilty that they change their minds.

AND I have ideas about how you can still hang out with pets even if you have tried lots of clever persuading and your parents still say NO (boo...).

Here is my stuff.

# Persuading your parents

✱ If you have parents who say NO to pets then don't try to persuade them to let you have a complicated pet like a snake or a squirrel 'cause then they will just laugh at you and say NO a bit louder.

✷ When you start begging for a sensible sort of pet it is a good idea to prove to your parents that you are a tip-top expert on that animal and know 17 million things about it.

✷ Drop clever things like "Did you know hamsters have expandable cheek pouches?" into the conversation even if you weren't talking about hamsters or whatever just so they know how much you know.

✷ Never take anything except pet-care books home from the school library – and be sure to leave them lying around your flat or house or wherever you live.

Whenever your parents walk into the room pretend to be reading the pet-care book even if you have really been looking at cool websites or watching **Dr Who**.

Try to look excited but then a bit sad every time you see your dream pet in the street or on TV or somewhere.

Write a contract that says you promise on all the pocket money in the world that you absolutely would look after a pet and not leave it to your mum to clean out its cage when it got a bit smelly or whatever. Sign it and be sure to include a bit that says if you break the contract your parents don't have to give you pocket money again in your whole life EVER (just to show how really serious you are).

# Fake your own pet

If you absolutely aren't allowed a real live pet (boo) then you could get a big soft toy and pretend it's real but that is just kids' stuff and kind of corny.

So here's my idea: I got bored one day 'cause I was supposed to go round to Indie's but she had diarrhoea and I couldn't oops I don't think she wanted me to say that bit about her having diarrhoea. Anyway she was sick and I was sort of sad that I couldn't see her and the dogs and Smudge the cat and it was raining and Mum said "Can't you find something to do?" so I made a fake pet.

## YOU WILL NEED:

- An old pillow
- Four socks
- Some safety-pins

- A black marker pen or wash-out-able felt pen if you think your mum will kill you for drawing on the pillow

- Some rubber gloves

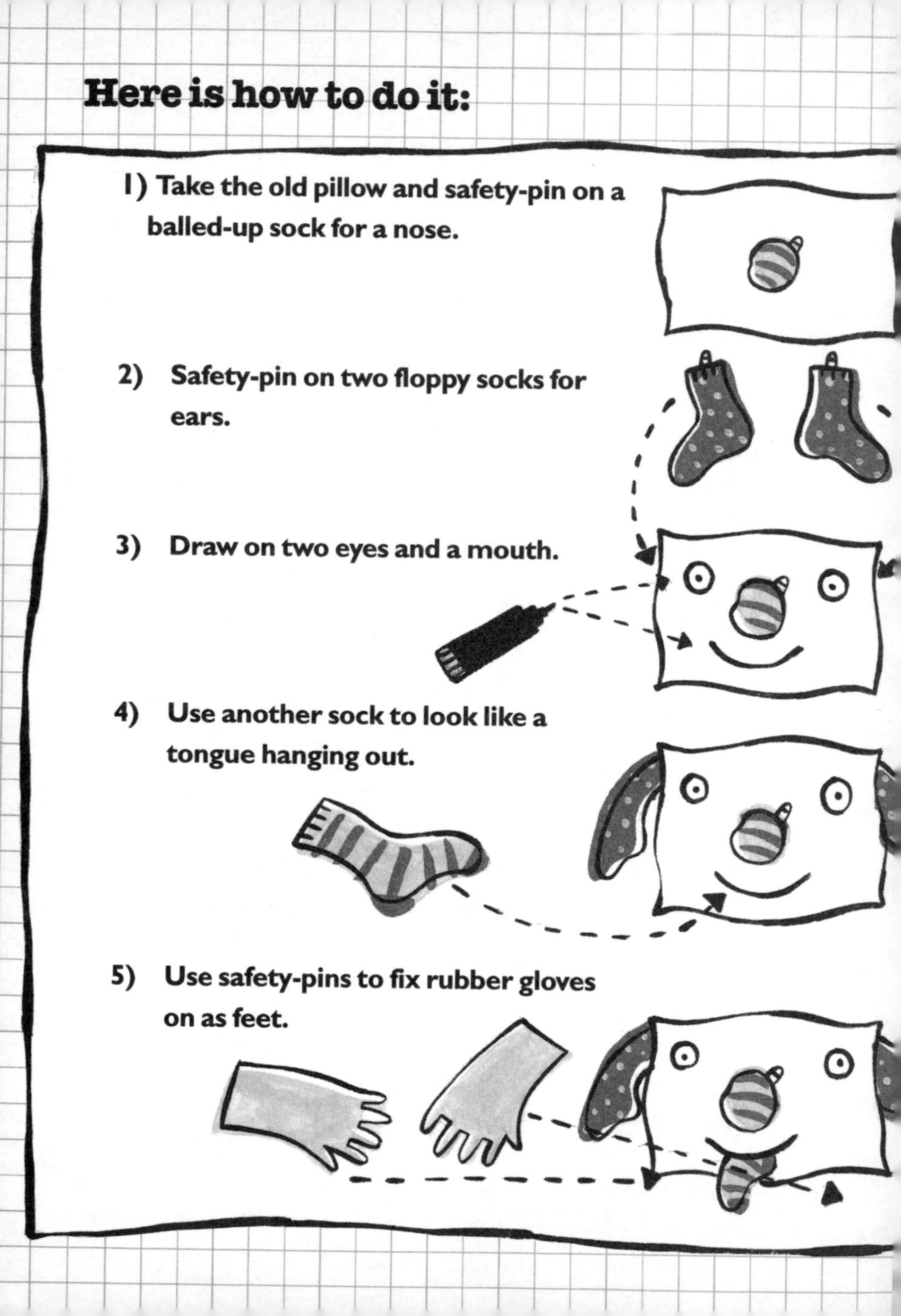
Here is how to do it:
1) Take the old pillow and safety-pin on a balled-up sock for a nose.
2) Safety-pin on two floppy socks for ears.
3) Draw on two eyes and a mouth.
4) Use another sock to look like a tongue hanging out.
5) Use safety-pins to fix rubber gloves on as feet.

6) Call your "pet" a wimblyosapus or a zebraphant or something dumb and cute.

7) Show it to your parents and make them laugh or maybe say "Ahhhhhh isn't that sweet..."

8) Keep your fingers crossed that your parents feel either so warm and fuzzy inside 'cause you made such a funny thing OR maybe so sorry for you (and a bit guilty that you are desperate enough to have made such a dumb thing) that they will change their minds and take you to the pet shop the very next morning if not sooner.

If your mum or dad or whoever you live with says I have seen your pet-care books and sad face and I know you know 17 million facts about this animal (and even smiles a bit at your wimblyosapus) but still says "NO you are not getting a pet" then maybe you will have to give up (for a little while).

**Four things you could do instead:**

**1)** You could make friends with someone at school who has a nice pet and hang out at their house a lot and help them with their pet. (I hang out at Indie's lots and it is excellent because they often have extra animals that Indie's mum takes home from the Rescue Centre to look after like baby hedgehogs.)

**2)** If your school has a pet you could look after it during the holidays (and then just sort of "forget" to take it back ha ha).

**3)** See if there's a neighbour who needs help with their pet. Indie says older people might have a dog that needs to be walked lots but older people's legs get too tired to do such a lot of walking so you could maybe offer to do it at weekends.

**4)** If there are any petting zoos or city farms or real farms or animal rescue centres near where you live then maybe you could help out on Saturdays or in school holidays. And maybe if you do that and come home and tell your mum and dad or whoever that you spent all your time cleaning out different types of poo for the whole time and you STILL had a good time then they will eventually think that you would be an ace pet-owner after all.

That is the end of my bit.

Except that I must tell you that I have lots of pet-care books about chinchillas lying around the house and I have a fake pet and it is called a fluffalupagus and Indie's mum says that I can come and help out at the Paws For Thought Rescue Centre when I am ten.

Thank you and goodbye from

Dylan Brookes

# Thanks to...

I couldn't have done this Pet Project without the help of the following people (and pets):

**Mum:** Because she is completely excellent, and the inside of her head is rather like an animal encyclopaedia. (Even if the outside of her head – i.e. her hair – usually has tufts of fur and hamster bedding stuck to it.)

**Amy the vet:** For lots of very good animal-care tips and stories.

**Dylan:** 'Cause I did lots of research for my project on his computer when I was round at his place on Sunday afternoons. He helped lots, even though he said stupid stuff sometimes (which made me laugh, so that's OK). And thanks to him too for doing such a good job of his bit, even if it didn't have any commas.

**Soph:** For telling me the story about her nursery-school hamster, and doing a brilliant impression of what he looked like when they found him (I didn't know it was possible for a person to suck their cheeks in that much).

**Fee:** For telling me about **collective nouns**. Except I don't think I can show her my Pet Project in case she gets to the bits about her cats Garfield and Mrs Mumbles and gets in a huff with me.

**Dad:** For just being lovely. (Except he wasn't very lovely to his pet bee.)

**Fiona:** For always making lovely cakes and stuff, and for saying "Ooh, that's interesting!" when I told her stuff about the project, even though she is not keen on animals at all.

**caitlin:** For playing me a whole bunch of animal-related songs on her didgeridoo when I was writing my Pet Project up all neatly. (I liked "Wanna Be Like You-oo-oo" from *The Jungle Book* best.)

**Jamie Ross:** For putting all those stupid suggestions in my Dream Pet box at school. If he hadn't, I wouldn't have been able to write about fun stuff like manatees and meerkats.

But most of all, I'd like to thank …

**Kenneth, George, Dibbles, Smudge, One, Two, Three, Four, Five, Five-and-a-half and Brian:** For being the loveliest, cuddliest* pets a girl could have.

** Dylan's just pointed out that only five of my eleven pets are actually cuddly or in fact cuddle-able**.*

*** I bet Fee would tell me that "cuddle able" is not actually a real word.*

# **Wow, wow, WOW!!!**

Miss Levy just gave us our projects back and I got a tick, a star AND a smiley face – and you just don't get a higher mark than that!! *YESSSSS!!!*

And she gave Dylan's bit its own little face too (only a sad-looking one with the word "Commas?" right beside it).

Mum is taking me and Dylan out for doughnuts with sprinkles on to celebrate. Got to go – *yay!!*

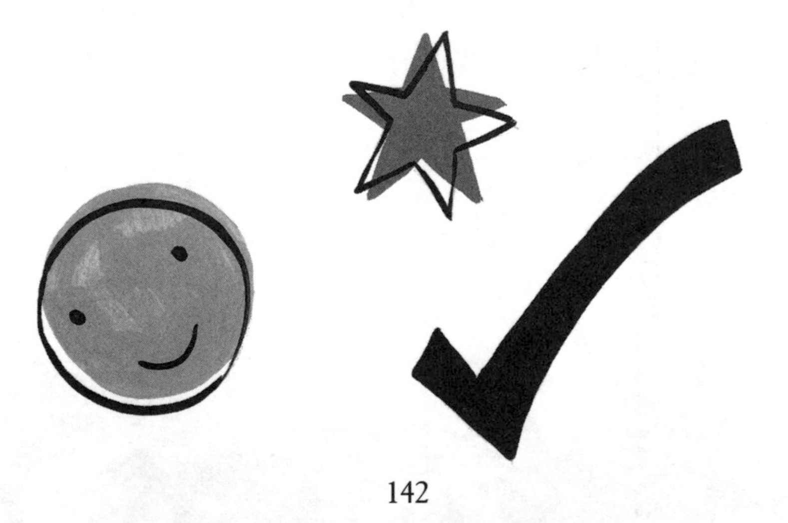